CHERRY ON TOP

A SEASONAL ROMANCE NOVELLA

JAYNE KINGSLEY

BLUEBERRY LANE
PUBLISHING

AUTHOR'S NOTE

Cherry On Top is a novella length sweet romance set in Washington D.C. during Spring.

At the end, I've included an except from another title in this series, A Kiss For Christmas Eve.

These books are connected by each having a seasonal theme, none of them feature recurring or related characters and all can be read as single titles.

ABOUT THE AUTHOR

Jayne Kingsley writes contemporary romance filled with fashionable and fun heroines and the hunky heroes that capture their hearts. She currently resides on the picturesque south coast of NSW with her two young daughters and her own real-life gorgeous hero.

She loves connecting with her readers. Head to www.jaynekingsley.com to sign up to her newsletter, or join her official facebook page.

1

—————

*A*deline Miller took a sip from the crystal glass in her hand. The champagne was ice cold and sprinkled her nose as bubbles burst with enthusiasm. She'd made it. The Pink Tie Gala was the start of her new life. Time to prove to everyone else she could do this. Prove it to two people in particular.

She allowed her gaze to travel about the room filled with Washington D.C.'s elite, all dressed to the nines and ready to kick off the Cherry Blossom Spring Festival. Adeline hadn't stepped a foot in Washington for exactly ten years. She mentally swiped at the thought as her mind sought memories from when she first left. Now was not the time for a trip down memory lane.

"Adeline?" A soft voice sounded behind her.

Oh no.

He wasn't supposed to be here. She'd checked the guest list. Twice. His name wasn't there, which was the only reason she'd ticked yes to coming tonight.

Taking a deep breath, she turned on the spot, the air whooshing out as her eyes met whiskey-brown depths. She stared, unable to pull her focus away before a slight bump from behind and a distant apology flicked the switch back on her brain. Taking another sip from her glass, she realized she'd finished the champagne. *Well done, Addie.* That was not quite the sophisticated image she'd been hoping to project.

Mason signaled a waiter, taking her empty glass and replacing it with a full one, his fingers brushing hers with a whisper touch, yet she still felt the sizzle all the way to her heart.

Ten years, and he still made her tremble like a schoolgirl?

She raised her chin. No longer was she that girl; she'd grown since she'd last seen him. Had rebuilt her heart and was stronger, at least she had been five minutes ago.

The silence stretched to an uncomfortable level, and Addie belatedly realized she hadn't even said one word to him.

"Mason." She nodded her head. Sophisticated, enigmatic. That's what she'd practised. What she told herself she would do if she saw him or her parents.

"I hoped I'd see you tonight."

His words threw her. He'd known she was coming? How did he know, especially since she hadn't seen his name on the list? Her confusion must have shown on her face, as his mouth quirked and he broke into a real smile.

"I'm guessing you weren't thinking the same? Hoping to avoid me again, perhaps?"

Well, he didn't have to act happy about that. His attitude took her right back into her teenage gawkiness, back to the eighteen-year-old pining after her older foster brother.

"Of course not. You caught me off guard, that's all. It's a pleasure to see you again." Bracing herself, she leaned in to brush her lips against his cheek and was enveloped by his masculine smell, which had really matured in the years since she'd last been this close to him.

When she'd thrown herself into his arms after too many glasses of cheap wine.

Best not focus on those memories, though it seemed it was too late to stop the slight pink tinge that rose in her cheeks. Whether it was at the memories or just being so close to the one man who had been her perfect ideal, against whom she'd compared all others, she wasn't sure.

"You look beautiful." His words were soft, wrapping around her like a warm blanket. She'd taken care choosing just the right outfit for tonight. The soft pink silk caressed her, the skirt flaring from the knee and allowing ease of movement. The dress color had called her name, like it perfectly matched the spring blossoms that were blooming all over the city. This was her favorite time of the year. She'd always loved cherry blossoms. As a little girl, she could remember running around the gardens during festival time. She'd begged her father to plant a cherry tree in their expansive yard, but he'd just laughed at her, saying it wouldn't suit.

Seeing Mason was making her think of her childhood, and why wouldn't it, given he was such a big part. Having him turn up at their family home one weekend, being told he would join their family... it had changed everything.

She focused on the bow tie of his jet-black tuxedo. It seemed the safer option than letting her gaze rove over how well it fit the rest of him. The silk of his bow tie matched her dress almost to perfection. Why did that bother her?

"You look different."

Her words made him laugh.

"Ten years, Adeline, did you really think I'd still be a

clumsy twenty-two-year-old?" His eyes twinkled with mirth. He was teasing her again.

"You were never clumsy." Her mouth twitched. She couldn't help it. Clumsiness had been 100% her thing, and he'd taken great delight in teasing her about that fact when they were growing up. Somehow, it had never seemed derogatory when he'd said it, unlike when they had teased her at school or when her parents had rolled their eyes at her inability to even walk down the street without tripping over something. When Mason teased her, it had been like their own personal joke. Surprise engulfed her that it still seemed to be the case. Something in his eyes told her he hadn't forgotten either.

"So, you're finally realizing your dreams?"

Her eyes darted to meet his. He remembered?

"That is why you're back in town isn't it? You're coordinating the final extravaganza of the Spring Festival? It seems to be quite the state secret but is gathering a lot of media interest. I'm proud of you. I know you've always wanted to work on a special event for the Cherry Blossom Festival."

Her mouth was strangely dry. Must be the champagne; it was acidic compared to the sweeter Prosecco she preferred.

"I..." her words hung unfinished, she herself unsure what she'd planned to say.

"You?"

"Senator, so glad you could join us after all. Though I must say I'm surprised given the circumstances." The snarky tone snapped the bubble Addie had been feeling with Mason. A burly man slapped Mason on the back, and his other hand guided a coiffed blond at his side. The man looked pleased with himself, barely registering Adeline standing there.

Senator? Her brows shot up, unable to contain her

surprise. She knew he'd gone into politics but hadn't known how far. She'd made it a point not to follow politics.

She didn't want to know.

The other couple moved away, leaving Mason with a scowl on his face. Was that because of her? Addie had smiled and nodded in the introductions but hadn't really been present enough to recall their names. Another failing she struggled to shake when in proximity of anything political.

Mason took her arm and guided them towards a quieter area of the room.

"You seem surprised?" His tone had an edge to it.

"By what?"

"By me being a senator. Surely your mother told you?"

Here we go. She'd hoped to avoid the topic of her parents, but it seemed her hopes were futile. Best just rip that patch off.

"We don't really talk much."

"I thought you would have buried the hatchet by now."

She shrugged, not wanting to encourage the discussion about her relationship, or lack thereof, with her parents.

"I take it you didn't know then. That I'm a senator? That I went into politics?"

She stopped walking, the pressure of his hand on her back adjusting before it fell away. She turned to look directly at him. "Look, Mason, I think it's great, but politics really aren't my thing."

"You still say that with a chip on your shoulder. Like it's my fault. That was one of the many things you threw at me all those years ago. Perhaps now we're both older, you'd care to explain? I would have thought that, as a senator's daughter, you'd show interest in the parties, in what's going on in your hometown?"

"Yes, well, politics was always more your thing, wasn't it? Yours and Dad's. No need for me."

She wanted to recall the childish words the moment they were out. This was not how she wanted this conversation to go. She'd worked her size-ten behind off to learn everything about event management and studied in New York under some of the best in the business. Her aim was always to come back and run a special event at the Cherry Blossom Festival, to fulfill a childish dream that highlighted so much for her. Her plan was not to come back and get involved in issues she'd put behind her. And definitely not have anything to do with the one man she needed to put behind her.

It wasn't fair that, all these years later, he still made her heart beat faster just by looking at her, being near her, speaking her name.

"Adeline."

She loved that he used her full name, letting the sound linger on his lips. It had made her sing with warmth back then, and unfortunately, it still did now.

He was right, much as she'd tried to dislodge it, the chip was still well and truly wedged on her shoulder, both shoulders if she was being honest. Her whole being vibrated with regret, and she still felt like she was coming up short.

2

Mason couldn't take his eyes off the woman before him. How she'd changed, had flourished into a stunningly beautiful woman. Her beseeching eyes hadn't changed though, the image of them burning with innocent desire was imbedded in his brain, haunting him. Back then she'd been eighteen, far too young. And he'd been the older, apparently wiser party. Not that it had ended well. She'd run away, and he'd always wondered if it was his fault, if he'd caused this rift with her parents. Her parents who had saved him, given him the life he had today, and he'd repaid them by alienating their only child.

He needed to make this right.

Dogged determination had earned him a seat at the political table, now it was time to put that into use mending Adeline's fences. Maybe then he could forgive himself and move on.

"So, what's the big secret event that's dragged you out of hiding in New York?"

He knew pursuing the conversation about her parents wouldn't work now. She'd clammed up, locked down those shutters she hid within her soul. He knew her well enough to know that when she didn't want to discuss something, she was stubborn as a mule. He'd need a new tactic to bring that out of her.

He didn't want to believe so much time had passed that he couldn't still be the one person who could get her to talk.

"I'm not hiding in New York."

Well, that worked; now instead of closed off, she was indignant. Annoyance at his comment had her finely arched brows knitted together on her forehead. He wanted to smile at her quick change in demeanor but didn't dare give his endgame away.

"Okay, I'll let that go for now. But the event? C'mon, Adeline, I'd love to hear about it. I remember spending countless hours sitting out in the yard whilst you pitched various ideas to a fictitious committee board. What has ten years of experience brought to your ideas now?"

It had been their ritual Sunday afternoon event. He'd sit under the old oak tree, and she'd stand before him, clipboard of scribbles, images, and drawings all neatly packaged, and she'd present her latest idea. Sometimes they varied, sometimes they didn't. But what never varied was her passion for the event. It shone like a bubble around her. He'd never thought to question why she'd loved it so much back then. Now it made him wonder: what significance did the festival hold for her?

He wasn't kidding. He really wanted to know what her winning pitch was. He knew how important running this event was to her, what it could do for her career. Her ideas as a child had been winsome and idealistic, but he imagined that, over time, they had evolved into more wonderful and sophisticated plans.

Her head dipped forward, a self-conscious smile gracing

her features. A few wavy locks of rich chocolate hair slid to frame her face, perhaps to hide another blush? He didn't know. She seemed to have an internal struggle before pulling herself together again, straightening and flicking the hair back out of the way. The whole maneuver would only have taken a minute, but standing as he was, inhaling her every feature, it felt like longer. It felt like a lifetime. Just another memory of Adeline he'd add to his lifelong struggle to resist the beautiful daughter of the parents who saved him.

Enough. He'd put those thoughts behind him. At least he thought he had. His goal tonight was to mend fences. From the moment he'd heard that Adeline had won the pitch and would be at this event, he'd known he had to do whatever he could to make things right. To fix the problem he'd created. He'd had to leave one of his own problems dangling, but he'd deal with that later. She needed to come first.

It should be him living out his life elsewhere, away from the Millers.

Not her.

"Okay, so you won't tell me about your plans yet, then how about a dance? We can catch up?" He held his hand out, waiting.

Now why the heck had he suggested that?

Her face registered surprise and then wariness. His own heart skipped a beat, waiting for her answer.

Her manicured hand slipped into his larger one. Her fingers felt smooth and cool, while his felt clammy and clumsy. She was a shocking dancer, but he knew she loved it.

Ugh, when would the memories of her stop.

"Worried for your toes."

It wasn't a question. Her eyes were bright, lit with humour he could only assume was aimed at him and his folly in asking her to dance.

He cleared his throat slightly. "Not at all."

He glanced down, hoping to see what kind of footwear she was wearing, deciding what damage she was likely to do. A glimpse of painted toenail glinted at him before the silk of her skirt swished it away. Open-toe shoes then, probably with stiletto heels. Her next step confirmed his suspicions.

His wince received a light-hearted giggle. "You asked me to dance. To answer your question from earlier, the answer is no, I won't be divulging any details of the event. It's top secret, and I plan to keep it that way until all is revealed on closing afternoon."

"Sounds mysterious."

"No, I want it to amaze people."

"I'm not people. C'mon, Addie, I'm your brother." He choked internally on the word. He'd never liked calling himself her brother.

He felt her stiffen. She'd been melting into his embrace, relaxing. But his words had shattered that feeling, leaving them standing in front of each other in a loose dance clasp but not moving. Couples swept around them. The music still played its soft jazz tunes. But she looked at him, accusation rife across her face.

"You're not my brother."

While her face was full of expression, her words lacked any tone, flat and impersonal.

She excused herself and walked away, leaving Mason standing alone on the dance floor. He looked around for the nearest wall he could bang his head against for a while.

Well, that went well.

3

———

*A*deline tried to put the memory of last night's gala from her mind. Again. She didn't want to think about it. Didn't want to think of all the memories and feelings that had rushed back when face-to-face with Mason.

Mason Smith. Her foster brother.

God, she hated that term.

He wasn't her brother. It didn't feel right to call him a brother. It never had. Oh, she'd idolized him, had followed him like a puppy when he'd first arrived at their beautiful white-brick home in Washington D.C. When she was a little older and her teen gawkiness stage had really kicked in, she'd moved into adoring territory. Then when puberty had hit her full on, and she was on the cusp of being a woman, she'd realized she loved him.

Except to him, she was just his sister.

The word made her sick.

"Adeline? Hello? Anyone home?"

She shook herself, realizing that she wasn't alone in her temporary office at Cherry Blossom Festival headquarters.

"Caroline, sorry, I was a million miles away. How can I

help you?" The PA assigned to the special-events team had a good poker face, not saying a thing about Adeline's lack of concentration.

"You have a call on line five? I tried to patch it through, but you didn't pick up. Did you hear the phone ring? I'm just asking because I'll get IT up to check it if you didn't."

Had her phone rung? Yikes, she had no idea.

"Maybe get IT up; I wouldn't want to be missing calls. So much to do at the moment!" Her overly enthusiastic voice sounded brittle as opposed to the cheery tone she'd been aiming for. Time to get her head back to the task at hand—putting on the best Cherry Blossom Festival end event. It would be fantastic even if she said so herself.

"Line five, you said?"

Picking up the handle, she pressed the middle button, offering Caroline a farewell smile as the PA left the office, closing the door behind her.

"Adeline Miller," she said into the phone.

There was a pause, but before the person on the other end spoke, she knew it was Mason.

"I'm just calling to apologize. About last night. I didn't mean to annoy you."

"You didn't annoy me."

"Liar, liar..."

"Mason, what are you, twelve? Though since I have you on the phone, I do want to apologize for walking off and leaving you on the dance floor. That was rude, and I'm sorry."

There, apology out of the way. She sounded calm and composed, mature, as opposed to her minor tantrum of last night. Cringing at the memory again, she shoved it away. It had been on repeat in her mind all last night, and this morning, she'd promised herself in the mirror that she'd thought of it for the last time.

"You need not apologize, Adeline. I was pushing you. I guess I was hoping we could talk about a few things, since you're in town?"

"What do you want to talk about? We're talking now, so shoot."

"I was thinking we could talk in person. Catch up properly. I could take you to lunch to celebrate your imminent success."

Lunch? With just Mason? Phone conversations she could handle. Not being within his proximity really helped her brain function at normal levels. But being around him? Seeing that smile, the whiskey-brown eyes she had dedicated hours of her life to memorizing? She was here to do a job, not fall back down the rabbit hole of Mason Smith, the unattainable man.

"I can hear the cogs of your mind turning, thinking, and I'm sure searching for a way out of lunch. But I'm not having it, Adeline. You've been avoiding your family for ten years, and it seems like it's my fault. I'd like you to hear me out. How's tomorrow at 1 P.M.?"

Confusion warred with shock inside her. He was being so direct, issuing orders. He'd never been like that with her previously. And his comments about it being his fault?

"Let me check my planner. I'm really busy with final preparations for the show, which is why I was pausing. I'm not avoiding you." *Liar liar, pants on fire.*

The planner was hidden under a stack of papers and took a while to locate. Flicking to tomorrow's page, there was a blindingly obvious gap in the day's middle. No previous engagement to call upon. The list at the top of the page was long, and the additional post-it notes told her she had a lot to do tomorrow, not that she needed her planner to tell her that, but she didn't really have any reason to say no to lunch.

"Seems you're in luck. I can do 1 P.M. Can we meet at Clovelly's? I need to go check a few things on location near there."

"Done. I'll make a reservation and see you there. Until tomorrow, Adeline."

He hung up. Adeline held the phone against her ear for a moment before dropping it back into the cradle. She couldn't be sure having lunch with Mason would do much for her fragile heart, but she hadn't been able to dismiss the determination in his tone, or his strange comments about him causing her to leave town.

Taking out a purple post-it note, her code for personal, she jotted down the details of her lunch date with Mason and stuck it in her planner. Lunch date.

Had she really just written the word *date*? It wasn't a date.

Picking up a black marker she drew a line through the word.

4
———

Mason drummed his fingers against the white-linen tablecloth. He hadn't expected Adeline to welcome his suggestion of lunch, but he also hadn't expected her to be so against the idea.

Ten years.

It had been ten years, yet it still felt like yesterday when she'd wound those slim arms around his neck and pulled him in for a kiss. A kiss that was a mixture of inebriety, courage, and young passion. A kiss he'd desperately wanted to return, yet knew he'd never be able to. Not then anyway.

He sensed her come into the restaurant before he saw her. The air in the room always changed when she was nearby. Like an extra breath of fresh air had entered his lungs.

Flattening his tie, he stood, ready to welcome her. Her eyes found his, skirting over meeting his gaze. Her lips were tight, and he noticed resignation and all the hallmarks of stress hanging about her as she stalked to their table. He wasn't sure if it was meeting him or her job that was the cause.

She'd looked amazing the other night, all wrapped in silk, her hair a cascade of chocolate waves spilling over her shoulder. Today, she was in business mode, not that the effect was any less potent. Her top must be some kind of silk from the way it danced about her torso, the top tied in a bow that should look ridiculous but which she pulled off. Her skirt was slim, hugging her curves and pulled in around her tiny waist. He imagined he could span that waist with his fingers, and the thought was enough to make him want to shove his hands deep into his pockets to hide from the temptation.

A coat was slung over her arm, covered with rain. "Adeline, good to see you."

He leaned in to brush a kiss against her cheek, breathing in her delicious perfume mixed with a scent that was just all Addie. Cherry blossoms. She'd always smelled like that. Previously, it had been innocent and intoxicating. Now it was simply intoxicating.

"It's raining." Her comment completely ignored his greeting, her tone bordering between fury and despair. He'd thought the little droplet of water on her check was rain, but perhaps not?

"Should I call the Coast Guard? Send out the Marines?" His attempt at humor was lame but helped him hold off the need to pull her in for an actual hug, even if she looked like that was exactly what she needed.

"It never rains in April."

He laughed; he couldn't help it. It was loud and burst forth unhindered.

"Seriously? We might have lost you to New York City, but surely you haven't forgotten how unpredictable the weather is here in spring. Heck, for all we know, it might snow tomorrow." He was joking, mostly.

She didn't appreciate it either way. Slumping into her chair, she ignored the waiter and Mason, who were hovering to help her be seated.

"Madam, the gentleman has ordered sparkling water; can I get anything for you or would you like a further few minutes to peruse the menu?"

"Anything but water. I don't need more water in my life. If the sky out there is anything to go by, water is about to ruin my life."

Mason's brows shot almost to his hairline. It felt ludicrous. The old Adeline had never been prone to melodrama; it was only a little rain, how was that ruining her life? He put aside the carefully crafted discussion points, apologies, and well, more apologies he'd planned to address during this lunch and instead waited for her to place her drink order before he raised a brow in question.

"It's raining, Mason."

"Yes, so you've said. A few times. I'm not sure I'm aware of the significance of this? It's only rain... isn't it?"

"My event is outdoors."

"So, use your wet weather backup option?"

There was a really long pause.

"I don't have one."

It came out mumbled as one word, taking him a while to sort out. "You don't have a wet weather option?"

He hadn't meant to sound so incredulous. Adeline had literally spent the entirety of her life, or at least as long as he'd known her, planning ideas for this event. And she hadn't thought to plan for the weather?

"It's a long story."

Concern flooded his whole body. "Shorten it for me."

She sighed. He could see it came from deep within, like it cost her mentally to even think.

"Well, you know I've always wanted this gig. That's no secret. But the pitch I put together, carefully crafted, painstakingly slaved over for hours, well, I couldn't use it. In the five minutes I had before pitching it, I found out someone else was pitching the same thing. I found out by accident, but it was too late to reschedule my appointment, so instead I came up with something on the spot. I sold it to the committee, and they ate it up. No one asked about weather options. I guess they didn't consider they'd have to, since I'm a professional and should have backup ideas for rain, hail, or a zombie invasion. But I don't, and honestly since getting the ok, I haven't had time to even think about it. I had to write the actual proposal, remember what the heck I'd said in the meeting, line up everything required to pull it off, and some of that, I'm still waiting to hear on. There just wasn't time. And now it's raining, and in eight days, if this rain doesn't clear up, my career, and lifelong dreams are toast. And worse than all, I'll ruin the festival."

She stopped to take a sip of her drink and then shrugged.

"So, that's the shortened version, and why the fact that it started raining as I left my office had me on the verge of crying. Don't you wish you were me? No, that's right, you're a senator, your dreams are already true."

Was that sarcasm? He couldn't tell. Or deflection maybe? She'd never liked to focus on talking about her problems. She'd clam up tighter than a stone if it was a problem involving her. If it was a problem involving any of her friends, well, she fought to the end to solve those.

She'd opened to him once, but he couldn't help her.

Perhaps now he could. He had connections, knew people in the right places. He wanted to address the black hole that lay between them, that used to be friendship and family, but maybe this would pave the way to filling that hole... It would mean putting aside his own work drama around the land tax bill. Senator Harris had taken great delight in implying Mason's decision not to go to New York and deal with the rumblings there had not gone in Mason's favor. He didn't regret canceling the trip, the opportunity to see Adeline... well, he couldn't live with himself on that front anymore. He wanted to make things right with her; she deserved that.

His phone beeped, signaling an incoming message. Another name who'd changed their mind about his bill. He felt a pang in his gut, worry that this issue was getting out of hand, but he'd have to deal with it later. He switched his phone off.

"Okay. Let's park the talk of dreams about to be torn apart and focus on what I can do to help."

She'd been studying the table setting before her, lost in her own thoughts, but his words had her head snapping up. Hope mixed with confusion flitted across her face.

"Why would you want to help me?"

Her words, spoken in a soft, small voice, broke him. Didn't she know, no matter what went on or what she thought of him, that he'd always be there to help her? He'd never really come to terms with calling her his sister, even though he'd used the word as a shield when he was younger, but he would always feel protective of her.

He scooped up her hand, giving it a squeeze. "We'll fix this, together."

5

———

Adeline didn't know what to say to Mason. She hadn't planned to share her worries with him. In fact, she'd planned to hear him out and then go back to having all ties with her family cut. She wasn't stupid; she had plenty of options she could switch to if the flood waters from above opened to rain on her parade. But they weren't as good as the idea she'd pitched. She knew the committee would accept last-minute changes if that's what had to happen, but it wouldn't have the same magical appeal.

Her idea was one that had always circled in her mind, like a dream she often woke up from. A ballet performance: a combination of the Japanese royal ballet company and American ballet academy, coming together in a mixture of dance styles to music created just for the event. As a child, it had been a dream which she'd played out with dolls. As an adult, she'd used every connection she had to make it come true.

And she would not look a gift horse in the mouth and say no––Mason had connections she could really use right now.

"Why do you want to help me?"

"I think given the rush on your project, we might be best to concentrate on that before we delve into our complicated past. Mending fences was a big reason I asked you to lunch today, and it's still a priority for me, but I think this takes precedence, don't you? The fates of the Cherry Blossom Festival and Adeline Miller's big debut hang in the balance."

His grin was one-hundred percent dialed to cheeky and was infectious. Addie couldn't help returning a grin of her own. Mason in full happy mode was impossible to resist.

"Okay, project first. Who do you know in the town-planning sector? Because I need to build something."

He gave her a thoughtful look, eyes creased in thought. She knew that look; he was wracking his brains.

"I might know someone who can help. What do you need to build?"

"A stage out in the basin. It needs to be large, and I'll need some smaller floats for lighting and a walkway for the performers."

"That's a lot you're asking there. I'm not sure I want to know how you were planning to achieve that without knowing someone in the city-planning office."

"Well, I have a backup location, I just like this idea better."

"Is the backup location under cover?"

"Yes, but then anyone viewing the stage would be in the rain."

He laughed and looked at her like he was trying to find an answer to a question he couldn't put into words.

Their meals arrived, and Adeline dived into the glossy fettuccine carbonara. Skipping breakfast hadn't been her finest move, and a morning of three coffees and the stress of the rain had left her jittery. Never mind the stress of meeting Mason.

She, too, wanted to clear the air from their past. Talk about how she'd kissed him, how he'd rebuffed her...called her his sister, how he'd said it was wrong. The memory still made her cringe inside, how silly she'd acted, the insults she'd thrown his way, coupled with waking the next day, her head aching, and going downstairs to overhear her parents talking about how they could fix the situation, how Adeline's infatuation with Mason was becoming a problem for her father. A problem, that's what they'd called her.

Her chest ached, a deep piercing pain that was just as strong now, ten years later.

"Can I have a guess at which idea you pitched?" His voice had dropped, softer and full of emotion. They hadn't spoken through the meal, and Adeline realized that her bowl was now practically empty. She looked up at him.

Goosebumps rippled up and down her arms, nothing to do with the rain-spattered clothing she wore, and every-thing to do with the whiskey-brown eyes that were staring into her soul. She felt bare. Too many memories were attacking her, and she didn't want to sit here any longer with Mason. She was too afraid of what that would do to her but unable to break the connection.

A voice shattered the moment. "Can I get you anything else?"

She shook her head, in response to the waiter or to finally break the link she was feeling with Mason, she couldn't be sure.

"Wait, actually, yes, can we have the bill?"

Mason's help was a Godsend, but she couldn't spend any longer sitting here with him. It was too much.

Once the waiter moved away, she looked back at Mason,

who was still focused on her, like there hadn't been any kind of interruption, like he was still waiting for an answer to his statement. Did he expect one?

"I need to get back to the office. If you don't mind, I'll email you all the details I think you can help with my...stumbling blocks, so to speak."

"You don't want to toss around backup weather ideas?" The words 'like we used to' weren't said but they may as well have been.

"Thank you, Mason, but no. I'll work out the rest." She would. Even if it broke her, she would deal with this, make the show a success. No need to give Mason, and in turn her parents, any more reason to think she was an abject failure.

6

———

Mason reviewed the email on his tablet screen as the streets of Washington's Georgetown district whizzed past him. Adeline had kept it short and to the point. All business.

He shook his head. There'd be time for personal business later. Right now, he'd offered his help, and from the looks of this list, there wasn't anything that he couldn't make happen.

Right now, though, he wanted some answers. Fortunately, his decision to go see Adeline's parents wasn't out of the blue; he often made an appearance at their Georgian home on Friday afternoon.

Flicking the tablet case shut, he focused out the window. It was a beautiful area of Washington D.C. He could still remember the first time he'd been driven along these streets, scared but refusing to let it show. He was one of the lucky ones, having been chosen from the foster home by the great Jeffery Miller to go join his family. At the time, he'd never been sure if it hadn't been a publicity stunt to win votes, but deep down, Mason hadn't cared. Opportunities like this didn't come around that often for kids like him, so he'd damn well make the most of it.

He'd been ten. Old enough to know how lucky he'd scored with this new family. He'd known nothing about politics, but living with the Millers and seeing the good that Senator Miller was able to do had gripped something inside Mason. He'd lapped up every bit of information about politics he'd been able to get his hands on and had discovered a knack for talking to people.

Plus, as a bonus, when he'd arrived on the doorstep, the door had swung open to reveal a dimpled, grinning, curly-haired bubble of energy. Six-year-old Adeline had barely stopped to say hi before she'd dragged him inside and told him they would be the best of friends. Oh, and that she hoped he liked playing with dolls. He didn't, but he'd pretended for her.

He'd pretended a lot of things for Adeline Miller.

The car pulled up in front of a large Georgian house, pulling him out of the memory. The white-brick façade was pristine, no less so now than when he'd first arrived all those years ago. Today though, he wasn't intimidated. The Millers weren't going to kick him out, and while he carried a lot of guilt that he'd caused their daughter to run away, he felt a renewed energy that he'd right that wrong before the Cherry Blossom Festival finished.

The gate creaked slightly as he pushed it open, his footsteps a comforting sound against the red-brick mosaic pathway. As usual, he was excited by the small noises, the familiarity of them, being able to hear himself think. He loved Washington D.C., the thriving inner city, the political banter and hectic schedule. For years, that had kept him on his toes. But coming back here let him breath. In comparison, the Georgian-inspired house with Corinthian columns was his fresh air, his home. Georgetown wasn't that far from the city center, but it was an escape all the same.

He didn't bother knocking, instead using his key to let himself in. Hanging his overcoat on the coat stand just inside the front door, he proceeded through to the library.

As expected, Jeffery Miller sat in the cream floral armchair next to the softly burning fireplace, a book open on his lap, propped up by his right leg hooked over his left. If Mason had a dollar for every time he'd caught Jeffery in such a position, well, he'd be a rich man.

Icy blue eyes lifted and assessed him, eyes very similar in colour to Adeline's, yet very different in personality. Jeffery always appeared to be scrutinising the world around him, like it was a puzzle he hadn't yet solved. As a boy, that had fascinated and intimidated Mason. Now, he knew it was a good show of never letting his true feelings be on display. Jeffery Miller was a closed book, end of story.

"Mason. I wasn't expecting you so early; how is the bill shaping up? Do you think you'll get enough support?"

Straight into business, as usual. Mason couldn't stop the heavy feeling deep in his gut. The bill was sinking faster than the Titanic, but Mason didn't want to tell Jeffery that. For the first time in his political career, Mason was unsure of the outcome, and what's more, he was struggling to find the desire to do everything he could to fix this problem. Sitting across from Adeline at lunchtime, he'd known he could help fix her problem, or he could work twenty-four seven to fix his own. Why had he chosen her?

He wasn't ready to delve into those thoughts, so he hedged in his reply.

"Too early to call still. I've got a few more in the party to talk to, but it's a good bill. There is some opposition, but I'm hoping we can smooth that over. I left it with Mark to finish up. I was hoping Clarise would be around today too?"

It wasn't entirely untrue. After lunch, he'd switched his phone back on to call Mark and see what he could do as far as damage control went, and then he'd turned his phone back to silent. He could feel it vibrating but was choosing to ignore it. He'd hopped in a town car to come straight here, waiting eagerly in the meantime for Adeline's email, which had arrived shortly after.

"Clarise is out in the garden, fussing with her hydrangeas, I believe. Apparently, next door's are thriving, and she's convinced someone has poisoned hers."

Jeffery's look suggested he thought the whole situation was tiresome, but Mason knew not to comment. Clarise's love of gardening, combined with black thumbs and no patience, was a recipe for disaster, one everyone seemed to know except for her. But as Mason hoped to scrounge himself some of her famous cherry pie, he figured it was best to keep that thought to himself. Clarise might be a terrible gardener, but she more than made up for it in the kitchen. Her cherry pies were this side of heaven, and as she still considered him a 'growing boy', he always got seconds and extra cream.

His tummy rumbled at the thought.

"Mase, is that you?" a lilting voice came from the direction of the kitchen. Nodding at Jeffery, whose head was already buried back in his book, Mason went in search of Clarise instead. He figured it might be better to broach the subject of Adeline with her first anyway. A casual comment about running into Adeline at the Pink Tie ball would be enough to get Clarise into organisation gear.

He hadn't asked outright, but it seemed Adeline had

decided to keep this trip a secret from her parents. But he'd let her run for long enough. She'd accepted the help he'd freely offered, and he'd requested one favour in return. Now he just had to get Adeline's father on board.

7

The cherry trees were in full bloom. The sight was more beautiful than Adeline's memories, and she sucked in a deep breath, the air intense with the sweet aroma. How she'd missed this.

The path held a scattering of pale pink petals, brushed off the trees by the earlier random wind and rain. Her thoughts turned back to Mason. He'd held true to his promise so far; the list she'd emailed him was being ticked off in methodical and quick succession. Had she expected any less?

No.

But his request for payment of that help was steep: a family dinner at their old home. Adeline had been back to Washington a few times since she'd left, but she'd avoided going to her home in Georgetown. Had avoided her family.

But Mason was adamant on this point. Why? Why did he want her to have dinner as a so-called 'family' so much? So she could re-live her humiliation, knowing she sat at the table with loved ones who didn't love her back? Whose expectations she'd never been able to meet? Her father who chose his political career and image over her feelings...

Her face burned at the thought.

Why? Why after ten years couldn't she move past this feeling? She'd been in other romantic relationships and had never questioned her abilities at work or in her life in New York. What was it about being back here that brought it all crumbling to the ground? Her carefully built self-esteem, career, all of it seemed to be a stumbling block whenever she was in this city.

But she still loved it here.

Did that make her narcissistic?

She'd been tempted to return a flat *no* to Mason's request. But how could she? Mason was solving a lot of her problems; he was pulling favours to make work happen that she never could have achieved. Sure, the event would still go forward without his help, but it wouldn't have the same level of pizazz without the strings Mason was pulling for her.

She'd sensed his split-second hesitation before he'd offered his help. Maybe he hadn't really wanted to? She was tying herself in knots trying to work out what was going on in that mind of his.

A drop of rain plopped to the ground before her, and with her next step, she felt another drop on her shoulder. Prepared for the possibility of rain after carefully scouring the weather forecast app she'd installed on her phone to give her hourly updates, she lifted the pink umbrella she'd bought at a sidewalk stall. The pink matched the trees, a clever marketing tool, and clearly the vendor was doing well, since she wasn't the only one carrying one of his umbrellas.

She felt a heaviness in her legs as the rain began to fall faster, droplets turning to sheets of water lashing the path and garden around her. How had she gotten herself into this mess? She had dreamed of running this event, of coming back to the festival, celebrating a key event that had always stuck in her heart.

Now she had the opportunity, and she had staked her career on an idea that wasn't fully thought out. And why? Because it had been Mason's favorite? How he'd delighted in telling her it was her best idea yet, all those years ago.

It had been one of her last ideas, well, one of the last she'd shared with him anyway. Soon after her fourteenth birthday, Mason hadn't been able to meet with her on Sundays anymore. He'd been expected to go to the club with her father, to meet with her dad's other cronies and work colleagues. To discuss political rubbish. Her teeth gnashed at the thought, trying to hold at bay the pain that wanted to envelope her.

How did Mason expect her to handle dinner with her parents? With her father, after what he'd done? And why on earth was *Mason* the one trying to mend these bridges?

Part of her worried if that was her fault, since she'd accused him of taking her place in the family, that fateful night of their kiss. She'd had her first taste of wine, and it had emboldened her, made her feel she was invincible, desirable. It had made Mason's glances at her feel warm and gooey, like he felt the same way she did.

Gosh, how wrong had she been. The fallout of her clumsy attempts at her first passionate kiss had been monumental. The words he'd flung at her had stuck, branded in her mind. He hadn't felt the same way.

Her father's words the next day had put the final nail in the coffin of her decisions. She'd accept the position for university in New York. She'd accept her parents' help for payment, but then she'd pay them back and walk away. She had been determined to distance herself from them, to free them of her and her ruining their perfect family image. They'd made her feel like their dirty little secret, the daughter they'd never needed. So she left, making way for Mason, the son her father had desperately wanted.

A dark thought struck her. Was her accepting Mason's help now for her own career gain just as bad as what her father had done? No...surely not...he'd chosen his career over his family. Was she now choosing her career over her own principles? She'd made herself a promise to never go back; wasn't that what she was compromising by accepting Mason's terms?

Water soaking into the soft leather of her ballet shoes jolted her from her thoughts. A small lake had formed across the pathway that led to the Jefferson Memorial building and the Tidal Basin, the site of her upcoming extravaganza.

Could she really pull this off? Certainly not without Mason's help, which meant she'd had no choice but to agree to this dinner. She just hoped she could make it through unscathed. She'd placed enough stress on herself with this project; she didn't need more in the form of remarks from her father.

8
____

deline glanced at her watch. Ten minutes she'd been standing here, ten minutes of waiting at the front gate after the taxi had delivered her. This was getting ridiculous, even for her. Besides, her heels were starting to pinch from standing on the hard cobblestones. Why she'd thought it would be a good idea to go buy a new outfit for this dinner, she'd never know.

No, that wasn't right, she did know. She was power dressing. If she looked great, looked successful, she'd appear so. This was the strategic plan she'd formed in the few days she'd had since agreeing to this dinner.

Who was she kidding?

Her head jerked up at the sound of the door swinging open. Mason stood within the frame, one hand on the doorknob, the other casually slung in his suit pants' pocket. He was grinning.

"Are you ever planning to come in?"

Oh. Guess her sidewalk pep-talk hadn't gone unnoticed. Not exactly the start she'd been hoping for.

She squared her shoulders, pasting a bright smile into place.

"Of course. I just had a few emails I had to reply to."

"Right." He didn't believe her, she could tell from the growing amusement on his face. Anyone else grinning like that would look ridiculous, but Mason pulled it off with ease.

He stood watching as she walked up the path. She'd expected him to head back inside the house, or at least move in some way. But he simply watched until she was standing on the landing. Her last few steps had slowed, hesitation in each movement. His cologne floated on the soft breeze, wrapping around her, closely followed by him wrapping his arms around her. Not a casual greeting. This was a full enveloping, bringing her into his personal space, and it had her pulse skyrocketing. Her stress and worry over this dinner tripled. Her agitation at being back here took hold of her entire being, gluing her to the spot. How did he do that? How did he invade her space like that, rob her of the shield she'd spent the past ten minutes—no, the past ten *years*, if she was being honest with herself—attempting to put into place?

He broke away first, his hands squeezing her shoulders, eyes locking with hers.

She wanted to scream at him not to touch her, but the words wouldn't form past her dry lips. Instead she flicked her tongue out to wet them, the movement followed by Mason's gaze. The tension returned full force, but for different reasons this time. Now she wanted nothing more than to be folded back into his arms and to press her lips to his. To eradicate all thoughts and feelings, replaced only by instinct and desire.

"Adeline!"

She was jolted out of her fantasy by a new pair of arms grasping her in a hug, the punchy feminine perfume a give-away. She'd know her mom's perfume anywhere.

What had happened just now? Mason had looked... interested. She threw him a questioning glance, but he was avoiding looking at her now, stepping aside so Clarise could lead her into the house and out to the back deck. Her mom was talking, but Adeline struggled to focus.

The table was set for fine dining standard, and the smells emanating from the kitchen told Adeline she was in for a delectable feast. Her eyes travelled to Mason of their own accord, a rose tinge lighting her cheeks. Gosh it really was exactly like old times; she'd fallen headfirst back into a schoolgirl crush.

Her father would have a field day if he sensed this. No need to give him any further reason to ridicule her, to look at her with the revulsion she'd seen on his face all those years ago.

"It smells amazing, Mom, I hope it was no trouble."

Could she sound any more mundane? But perhaps that would be best, stick to safe topics. *Were* there any safe topics?

"Nonsense, it's never any trouble to cook a wonderful meal for all the special people in my life."

Taking Adeline's coat, her mother moved back inside. Her dad hadn't made an appearance yet, and Addie could only assume he was holing up in his library, avoiding as much small talk with her as possible. Her chest ached, and she rubbed a hand across the area to try and loosen the tightness that had formed there. She felt so conflicted. She didn't want to see her father; hours of her life had been dedicated to proving him wrong, not that he knew that. But part of her, the little girl that still lived inside her, wanted to show him he was wrong about her.

That really did make her a clumsy fool.

Adeline walked out to the back veranda. Happy to be alone for a moment, she moved to lean on the railing. It wasn't a high deck; only three stairs worth separated her from the rich green grass. The old oak tree still stood at the back fence, towering over the area. She'd always been drawn to that tree, even from a young age. Was it because it was as far as she could go without actually leaving the property?

Her mom loved her, she didn't doubt that. But she'd never reached any of the potential her father had hoped for, and deep down, she'd always felt like a failure to them. She'd been a bright and funny little girl who loved to dream but hadn't grasped any of the lessons they'd put her in. Her school grades had been abysmal, sports were a disaster area, and she was a girl. She knew her father had wanted a boy. No young child would ever forget hearing that they weren't 'living up to expectations.'

She sensed more than saw Mason arrive, just before a glass of chilled white wine was held in her periphery.

"Thanks," she murmured, accepting the glass and taking care not to touch his fingers.

The wine was dry and icy cold. She glanced over her shoulder, but the space behind Mason was empty. Another ache joined the first.

"He's just taking a call in the library."

Was she that obvious?

She offered a tight smile before taking another sip of her wine, hiding any further feelings. Mason didn't need any help reading her.

9

Mason was torn. Part of him wanted to wrap Adeline in another hug, to pull her into his arms and never let go. But that was the problem: he wasn't sure he'd ever let go. He needed to focus on mending this rift between Adeline and her parents. His personal apologies and request for forgiveness could wait.

Jeffery's timing on the phone call couldn't have been worse. Though to be fair, Adeline had stood outside the house for quite a while. He was watching for her taxi, partly because he hadn't been sure she'd actually turn up, but she'd said she'd be there, and she had come. Except she'd stood outside on the pavement like she was arguing with herself. For a while, he'd just watched, amused by her antics. But after a while, he worried she'd never come in unless he gave her a push. He hadn't meant to block her path at the doorway, to give her that hug, but he'd felt her pain in his heart like it was his own.

Now she had the same expression on her face. The smile was there, but behind it was nothing. Her mouth gave it away, the shape slightly different when she was smiling for real. Many years had passed, but her smile hadn't changed one bit.

Scolding rang from the kitchen, and Mason assumed Jeffrey was finally off his call and being ordered outside for dinner. Clarise had changed over the years; the serene senator's wife had morphed into a tyrant when it came to getting her husband to do as she asked. He'd asked her last year why she'd changed so much, and her answer had left him stunned. She'd never been any different; it was simply that now she didn't feel she had to express her demands in private. Jeffrey wasn't a senator anymore, wasn't public property, he was back to being all hers, and she'd say what she wanted to him. It still made him laugh. Clarise could be downright bossy when she wanted someone to do something.

He hoped she'd use that on Adeline today and push her to spend time here after the Festival.

Adeline tensed beside him. She was strung out like a fishing line with a barracuda on the end. Her dad's voice reached them before he appeared in the doorway, muttering something under his breath.

"Addie, thanks for making the time to come visit."

She winced. It was subtle, but he could pick up on it clearly. Her dad's tone had been friendly enough, but that wasn't his best choice of words.

"It's good to see you, Dad. I hope retirement is treating you well?"

"Yes, it's fine. Plenty of time for golf, I suppose."

"I didn't know you'd taken up golf, good for you."

Stilted. The whole conversation was stilted, like they were dancing around a fire and neither wanted to be burned. He needed to help clear the air.

"Jeffrey, you should hear Adeline's ideas for the end event of the festival. It's going to be spectacular."

Questioning blue eyes pinned him, narrowing slightly before breaking away when her father spoke.

"Of course, let's sit. Your mom is on the war path with this dinner, so we best follow her orders. Mason, you're to sit on this side with Adeline. According to Clarise, it will give you both the best view, and we'll be able to look at the two of you, giving us the best view."

Adeline choked on the sip of wine she'd been taking. Mason gave her a quick pat on the back, his hand lingering before he let it drop. It had been meant as a soothing gesture, but it sent his pulse up.

Clarise came out of the kitchen, a platter piled high with a variety of delicious-smelling food. It appeared she had created a tapas of sorts, not that Mason was any kind of food critic. If it was edible, he'd eat it. It was one of the few habits from when he was younger that he'd never been able to kick. A soft ache pinged around his heart. He didn't dwell on his time before he was welcomed into the Miller fold, but he'd never forgotten where he'd come from, or how lucky he was.

The crash reached his ears before he could register what had happened.

What was left of the platter lay in pieces on the floor, the bright splattered food almost artistic against the stained wood beneath it.

Clarise had tears in her eyes, Adeline had gone white as a sheet, and Jeffery looked ready to yell. Everyone had frozen, Clarise next to a half-crouched Adeline, who was wearing part of the platter on her cream dress.

"Still so clumsy!" Jeffery's words spat into the silence.

"Jeffery! It wasn't her fault. I was too busy showing off to look where I was going. We moved at the same time, is all."

He heard Adeline mumble something; he thought he caught the word *bathroom* but couldn't be sure, and then she took off inside the house. When she brushed past him, he saw her holding back tears.

Not exactly the start he'd hoped for. Hesitating for a moment, he followed Adeline inside. The downstairs bathroom door was closed, and he could hear running water through the door.

Knocking softly, he waited, and then tried the door to find it locked.

"Adeline?"

"Go away, Mason, please, I just need a moment."

Her voice sounded haggard, like it was underwater. Taking a step back, he leaned against the wall opposite. Given the start, he wouldn't blame her for leaving the bathroom and making a quiet escape.

After a while, the door opened, slowly revealing Adeline, who wouldn't meet his gaze. Her eyes were puffy and red rimmed.

"Why are you determined to push this, Mason?" Her words were quiet and full of strength, especially considering the rest of her looked as fragile as glass.

"Because they are your parents; they love you."

She scrunched up her nose at that comment.

"Look, Adeline, what happened all those years ago... you said something that's always stuck with me, you said you felt your parents saved me to replace you. I tried to contact you after you left, but you wouldn't take my calls, and I've always regretted that we didn't part as friends. You're part of this family. No one can replace you."

There was a long pause after his words. He could see her

thinking, expressions floating over her face from sadness to frustration and then back to a neutral mask.

"Mason, I'm really tired and under a lot of pressure right now, let's just get this dinner over with and save any deep conversation for another time. I was eighteen, I was drunk, I don't remember half of what I said to you that night. I was...hurting."

He could see that. She still wouldn't meet his eyes. He was amazed that she hadn't said she was leaving.

"Are you sure you want to stay?"

"I made a promise, Mason, I keep my promises."

The words felt like a kick in the gut. He wasn't sure why, but they did. He followed her back out to the veranda, where her parents were clutching glasses of wine, studiously avoiding each other. It seemed the conversation out here hadn't gone well either. He knew Clarise was desperate to form a link with Adeline again. He could imagine she was hurting at how the evening had gone so far.

Mason had to wonder if he'd done enough back then to try and fix the situation. He'd known Adeline was crushing on him, he'd tried to hold her at arm's length, but had he done enough? At eighteen, she'd been beautiful but also very much forbidden fruit. He owed her parents so much; he couldn't entertain the idea of a dalliance with their daughter.

"I'm sorry about the platter, Mom, it looked amazing."

Adeline's words jolted him from the past. The peace offering had Clarise jumping up, refusing to accept the apology. The hug they shared was awkward. It wasn't much, but it was a start.

"I can pop out and grab something from down the street?"

"I've ordered pizza. I hope you'll both stay." Clarise held

such hope in her voice, wringing her hands in front of her. Mason mentally willed Adeline to say yes but left the decision up to her.

"Okay...pizza sounds good." She looked at him then, for the first time since the platter debacle. Offering him a half-smile, she resumed her seat. Mason wanted to punch the air with the small victory.

Jeffery had sat stonily silent through the whole exchange, but he did lean forward and top off their wine glasses.

"Adeline, you were going to tell us about your project?" Mason spoke the words into the silence that was brewing. Anything to hold any further disasters at bay.

"Oh yes, Addie, please do! I always remember how much you loved the Cherry Blossom Festival, how you used to light up whenever March came. You'd bubble with excitement the whole month, asking daily if we could go into town. Jeffery, do you remember that dress Addie would always wear? Until the year it wouldn't fit her, gosh, I remember you crying buckets, darling, when we couldn't do the zipper up."

Mason had been smiling at Clarise, caught up in the memories. He knew just what dress she spoke of, a pale-green dress that had cherries stitched around the base. He glanced over at Adeline, expecting her to be smiling. Her lips were turned up as if she was smiling, but her eyes told a different story. Small creases had formed between her brows.

Did she not remember the dress?

Her next words were soft. "Yes, I remember the dress." She opened her mouth to say more and then closed it, hesitating briefly before she continued. "Do you really want to hear about the project?"

Clarise sent Jeffery a glare, and he hunched his shoulders before nodding his agreement. Jeffery watched his daughter as she slowly told them a little about the project and how she'd ended up with the contract. Mason thought he detected guilt on Jeffery's face at one stage... but why?

Clarise missed her daughter terribly. She'd never uttered the words, but Mason knew from her body language whenever Adeline's name was mentioned.

Jeffery was a stubborn so-and-so, and Mason knew firsthand he'd never been very encouraging of Adeline and how hard he'd been on her as a child. But the guilt surprised him.

He'd always wondered why Adeline's parents hadn't made a bigger effort to bring her home. It only dawned on him now that maybe he was missing something from this puzzle.

10

_A_deline gave her mother a kiss on the cheek, soaking in the familiar smell of her perfume before she waved farewell and walked down the steps. She'd agreed to meet her mother for coffee the following day. At the time, it had seemed natural to accept the invitation, but doubts crept in with every step she took away from the house.

Dinner had been a revelation, that was for sure. Her father had asked about her job. Had actually looked interested! During the meal, she thought she detected a hint of guilt and remorse in his expression.

Adeline had given up hope on mending the past with her parents. They'd said things, she'd said things...things she didn't feel she could take back. They hadn't supported her dream, at least, her father hadn't. And when he'd found out about her kissing Mason? Well...she'd never forget that look of disdain, the words he'd said, the choice he'd made.

After she'd left, her mom had phoned often to begin with, but those calls had dwindled after a few months, and each of them adopted the idea that the incident wouldn't be spoken about. That distance was for the best.

Adeline hadn't ever told anyone, but it hurt. It hurt that for years she'd felt essentially alone in the family department.

The air had a slight chill to it, clouds racing to cover the sun that was dwindling in the evening spring air. The jacket she wore was pretty light, and she pulled it tighter to ward off the erratic weather. Looked like more rain on the way.

A dull thud sounded in her belly at the thought. More rain.

"Adeline. Wait!"

She paused mid step, twisting on the spot to view Mason jogging towards her. He'd offered her a lift, but she'd lied, saying there was a taxi coming to collect her. She should have known he'd catch her out. At the time she'd just felt like walking, spending the time in her own head, trying to find some sense in everything.

Looking about, she realized she'd actually walked a fair distance.

"How did you find me?" She blurted the words, not meaning to sound accusatory, but it came out that way.

He was catching his breath, his torso puffing out against the white cotton of his shirt. The man was seriously fit, yet he looked like he'd just run a marathon.

His eyes danced away from hers. He cleared his throat, hesitating before he looked back her, a sheepish expression in place.

"Okay, you caught me, I tried to follow you. But it would seem I chose the wrong direction to begin with."

Disbelief bubbled inside her, a few giggles escaping and then escalating into all-out laughter. She didn't even know why she found this so funny; she just did.

"Sorry, I don't mean to laugh."

"Yes. I can see you're really trying to hold it in on my account."

Mason looked hot and ruffled, a look she could really get used to.

"So why did you follow me?"

"I wanted to check you were okay. *Are* you okay?"

"Oh."

She took her time in responding. Dinner had been a surreal experience, but she hadn't hated it. She wasn't about to book a moving truck to come back to Washington, but she felt more comfortable here than she had in a long time.

A bell rang along with an angry voice telling them to move. Mason grabbed her body and pulled her against him, out of the way of the bike that flew past.

Hard chest and sweaty masculine smell permeated her brain. Warmth spread from where Mason's hands gripped her back, and his fingers gentled their firm hold, but didn't move. She was pressed against him, layers of clothing separating them, but every tiny contact point springing to life. She took a deep breath but regretted the choice right away, his scent only enhancing the heat that was spreading throughout her.

"Adeline, are you okay?" His words were low, and sounded a little strangled, like he, too, was fighting this attraction.

Her gaze flicked up to his, icy blue meeting whiskey brown. Had she ever noticed he had little flecks of caramel in his eyes? She swallowed.

She opened her mouth to say something but didn't expect the words that came out. "I'd like you to kiss me."

Mason didn't wait to be asked a second time. He lowered his head, slowly inching that delicious mouth towards hers. His eyes never wavered from hers, like he was seeking reassurance she wouldn't change her mind. The wait was excruciating, and then finally it was over.

Soft lips pressed against hers, tentative, then with more force. She dived in, soaking in the dreamy satisfaction of kissing Mason and having him kissing her back. Memories hadn't done this justice, though she supposed they'd both grown a lot in the intervening years.

His hands cupped her cheeks. She missed their warmth on her back but having them cradling her face was so beautiful. She'd never felt this connected to someone before in her life. She lifted her own hands, placing them over his, linking their fingers.

He broke the kiss, placing a gentle kiss on her hand before resting his forehead against hers. His eyes locked with hers, searching, for what, she didn't know. Her lips lifted in a small smile.

"Thank you." She giggled. Why had she said that?

His eyes crinkled in return, yet he remained silent for a moment longer, just staring at her. His intensity was starting to make her squirm.

At last, he sighed and took a step back, keeping their fingers linked as their hands swung between them.

"I think maybe we need to talk before this goes any further."

Well, that didn't sound good. Her brows knitted together.

As if reading her thoughts, he said, "Nothing bad, just... I don't want to complicate this... I want to see you, a lot, but I was to blame for your leaving last time. I really want to fix that situation before we become anything else to each other."

She pulled her hands away, folding them over her chest.

Unsure how to respond, she was saved by the ringing of her phone.

"Sorry, I have to get this." Digging in her bag, she found the phone somewhere near the bottom, swiping the screen with her thumb as she brought it to her ear.

Her assistant's voice came through, updating her on the festival progress. Nodding her head, she mumbled some form of response before saying she'd see her first thing in the morning.

"Mason, I need to go. Um, can we talk after the festival is over? I just...I have so much going on right now."

She needed time to sort through the thoughts in her mind before speaking to Mason. The kiss was magical, but she needed to come clean to Mason about the real reason she'd been staying away.

He'd been watching her throughout the call, his expression inscrutable. He narrowed his eyes, a slight frown forming. He wasn't buying it, she could tell. But she knew he was right, they did need to talk before this became anything else.

Trouble was, Addie just didn't know where to start.

11

Mason slammed his office phone down. This situation was getting out of hand. The bill should have been easy, but instead it was falling apart with every phone call he'd received. While he'd been racing around trying to fix Adeline's problems, he'd left his own to blow up. He'd been receiving funny looks from his staff all morning, being asked questions he had no answers too...this wasn't like him. In all the years he'd been in politics, he'd never put a foot wrong, never dropped the proverbial ball. Now he wasn't only dropping it, he was practically on the field running towards the opponent's goal.

He needed to fix things. But he couldn't get his head to focus. The kiss with Adeline yesterday swirled in his brain and just wouldn't be ignored. He wanted to talk to her now, not hold off until after the festival. This feeling of being in limbo, of not knowing where he stood, brought back a bucketload of baggage from his youth. He generally avoided uncertain situations like the plague. Is that why it had taken him so long to try and fix the rift he'd seen form between Adeline and her parents?

Tim, one of Mason's staff, poked his head through the door.

"Mason, we have another problem. Senator Davids has just pulled his support too."

A lump formed in Mason's stomach. Davids was one of his main supporters, one of the main players in this game. If they lost his support, the bill was done.

"Get him on the phone for me please, Tim? Let's see if I can fix this situation."

Tim hesitated, looking unsure whether to speak his next words. "Mason, is something going on? You've got people worried."

Yes, he could see people were worried, himself included. "I'll fix it Tim, just get him on the phone will you, please?"

Stress weighed him down, but he wouldn't let it show. Davids knew something was up; Mason just hoped it wasn't too late to find out what he'd missed and turn the tide back in his favor.

The call was short and left Mason feeling numb as he hung up the phone. His decision to not go to New York, a last-minute decision he'd made the moment he'd seen Adeline Miller's name on the guest list of the ball, was now a serious problem.

His problem.

There were no answers to this.

His cell phone beeped, a text confirming the last task on Adeline's wish list. He brightened slightly when he read the words. Assuming the rain held off, she'd be able to proceed with her original plans.

Typing out a quick message, he passed on the good news, before tossing his cell phone back onto the stack of papers before him. He's spent months putting this deal together. It was going to be a big shining point in his political career.

He expected to feel a lot worse, and his brows knitted over the reason why. A face popped into his mind, Adeline's, looking at him like he'd just offered her the world.

Standing, he slid the suit jacket off the back of his chair, slipping his arms into the sleeves. He buttoned the jacket, straightened his tie and took a deep breath. A walk to clear his thoughts was what he needed.

He'd chosen to help Adeline instead of focusing on his deal.

Why?

He discarded the idea that it was guilt. Sure, some of it was that he wanted to compensate her for feeling like he'd taken her place in the family. But over the years he'd tried to reason that out, and he couldn't really be blamed for that. Jeffery had never supported Adeline. That wasn't on Mason.

But Mason should have fought harder to see her, to keep in contact. That *was* on him.

If this decision wasn't all guilt, then what was it?

He'd managed to avoid speaking to anyone as he left the building, for which he was thankful. His head was a turmoil of thoughts. When the fresh air hit his face, he took a deep breath and immediately felt lighter. It was a little cool outside, and if the cloudy skies had anything to say, they'd likely get some rain soon.

He flagged a cab and asked to be taken to the Tidal Basin. He didn't dwell on why he'd chosen that location. Once there, he handed over the fare to the cabbie and then stepped out, the air vibrant with the smell of cherry blossoms. Choosing the path that led down to the river, past the Jefferson Memorial building, he shoved his hands in his pockets and adopted a casual stroll. A group of joggers passed him, their collective heavy breathing and chatter reminding him he wasn't alone. In fact, there were people everywhere, most of them with cameras or iPads, taking pictures of the cherry blossoms that were in full bloom.

He had to admit it was a sight to be seen. Delicate flowers in at least ten different shades of pink hung in clusters, like clouds bunching around the skyline. If you looked up, it was just a sea of pink. A slight breeze had a selection of petals floating off the tree closest to him.

The beauty of it touched even him; no wonder it was such a fascination to Adeline. He could picture her as a young girl, running around in the petals. She'd been a fresh-faced eighteen-year-old the last year they'd gone to the festival, and she'd still danced under the trees, her hair cut short in a sophisticated bob. The style had really suited her and had shown off her slim neck.

A jolt at his shoulder make him realize he'd stopped walking and was standing at the edge of the path, blocking other people's way.

He shook off the memories before he resumed his walk. This outing was to work out a way to solve his political situation, not to reminisce over Adeline.

Veering off the main path, he headed away from where the crowds were congregating towards the memorial. He could still reach the water this way, but he wouldn't need to fight with loads of people and cause any more pedestrian malfunctions.

The trees were sparser here, as were the people. He spotted a park bench, a woman dressed in bright pink sat on the edge, leaning down towards...was that a squirrel? He squinted. It really looked like that woman was talking to a squirrel.

He was about to change direction when the woman sat up, and as he recognized her, he wondered if he'd conjured her into life. He lips stretched in a smile, unable to stop the soft laugh that escaped.

Adeline glanced up, a lopsided grin gracing her features. The squirrel gathered up something before it scampered up into the closest tree. She stood, brushing down the skirt of her dress.

The move was casual, but something about it hit him in the gut.

Her hand lifted in a half-greeting as she walked towards him.

He cocked his head to the side, waiting until she stood before him. "Sorry I interrupted your conversation."

Her cheeks heated, and she ducked her head before looking towards the tree her friend had run up.

Another bubble burst inside him. He'd left the office to think, to try and fix his problem, to work out why he didn't seem as concerned as he should over the fact he'd chosen to solve Adeline's problems instead of focusing on his own. Standing before her now, watching her worry her bottom lip, probably trying to think of some explanation for being caught talking to rodents, all he could think of was that he wanted to taste those lips. He wanted to kiss her, and hold her, and never let her go.

His heart skipped a beat, his thoughts clear.

He loved her.

"Okay, this is going to sound silly, but I was asking him if he'd mind maybe praying for no rain. To be honest, I've been asking the trees as well. They are all nature, so maybe they have some special link to the weather. Gosh, Mason, I don't know. I suppose the stress of tomorrow is getting to me. Do you think I'm losing it?"

He loved Adeline Miller.

She was looking at him. He'd heard her words, and her voice had floated on the periphery of his focus, but his own thoughts overrode anything she'd said. He was in love with her. All these years later, his feelings had blossomed, from attraction back then to falling for the woman who stood before him now. It had only taken a week, but he knew, soul deep, he knew.

He needed to say something. She was looking at him in concern, her eyes trying to capture his, a frown across her features.

"Sorry. I..." It wasn't often that he couldn't think of something to say. Words were his tool; his mind and his words were what got him this far, why were they now deserting him.

"You're stumped. I get it. I guess watching someone talk to a squirrel would do that. Let's just pretend you didn't see it, and we'll move on."

"Yes. Let's." Conversational genius there, Mason.

"I got your message. Thanks for sorting out the pontoon and licensing. I was worried the dancers were going to end up having to actually dance on water. Wasn't sure how I was going to make that work, really."

She was babbling, which suited him just fine. His earlier revelation was still sinking in.

"Mason, is something the matter? I mean other than you discovering I'm going mad?" She laughed self-consciously. Her words flippant, but he could sense the real concern under them. Her fingers brushed his arm, the touch light.

Yes, something was the matter. He'd just worked out he was in love with her. Adeline was about to fulfil her dreams, and was starting to mend fences with her parents. Not to mention that her life was in another state. He couldn't tell her. Not now. But he needed to tell her something.

"I've lost the bill. It goes to vote tomorrow and the supporters we were counting on to get it passed have backed out."

"Oh, Mason, I'm so sorry. Why are they backing out?" Her hand reached out again, this time clutching his arm, the contact soothing.

He shrugged, not wanting to get into the details, given Adeline hated politics. He should really find someone else to talk to. Except...it was her he wanted to talk to. His thoughts must have been clear as day on his face.

"You can tell me. I know I'm the first to tune out when it's anything political, but you've really come through for me this past week, Mason. And I'd like to be there for you. Maybe talking will help?"

He took a deep breath, letting it out in a whoosh. He felt a warmth radiating from Adeline's hand on his arm, from the connection.

"It's my fault. I needed to go see someone in New York, and at the last minute, I pulled out. I didn't think through the consequences."

Her thumb rubbed against the hairs on his skin. Her fingers were so smooth. "Can't you go see them now?"

He was glad she hadn't asked why he'd pulled out.

"No, the opportunity from that source has gone. There will be other bills. I just feel terrible that I've let my team down. They've worked really hard on putting this together; it was pretty much all wrapped up, and I've ruined it."

"Mason, I think you're being a bit hard on yourself. You haven't let your team down, this is the game of politics. Sometimes votes go your way, sometimes they don't. Gosh, remember when Dad was trying to get the new tax laws passed? He thought it was all a done deal, and then bam, it went south. He was livid. Have you spoken to him about this? Maybe he knows someone who can help."

It wasn't a terrible suggestion. He didn't know why he hadn't thought of that sooner. Actually, he did know: he was distracted and wasn't thinking straight. If there was one last hope to get this turned around, Jeffery was it. Then another thought occurred to him.

"You should ask him."

Adeline looked at him like he'd lost his marbles.

"Seriously, Adeline, you should call your father and ask. You said you owed me for all the help with the festival. Well, this is how you can repay me. Call your father."

"No way. Dinner the other night was your payment. You can't just keep using that."

"Okay, you're right. But I think it would mean a lot to him if you reached out."

"And if he can't help?"

"If he can't help, well, the bill is dead in the water at the moment anyway. To be honest, I should feel worse about that, but I don't. What would make it better though, would be knowing you and your father are at least trying to work things out."

"Why are you so hell bent on trying to fix things between my parents and I?"

"Because it's my fault." The words cost him. They came from a place deep down, knowing that this was going to open a can of worms. But he'd been hiding from this conversation, not wanting to rock the boat and ruin the perfect life he'd been living, which wasn't fair to Adeline. At the time, he might have convinced himself it was for the best, that if she was in New York, he wouldn't be tempted to fall for her charms, any more than he already had, but he hadn't expected her to dissolve all ties. For that he'd never forgiven himself.

Adeline took a loud, deep breath, hurt written across her features. "Mason, I know what I said to you all those years ago...it implied that your place in the family, your connection with my parents was the reason I left. I regret that I never corrected that. Part of my leaving...sure, I was embarrassed by how I'd acted around you, knowing you felt nothing at all for me other than considering me your sister and there I was throwing myself at you in all my teenage hormonal glory. I was young, and my reaction was immature. But you aren't the reason I left and have been avoiding coming back."

Heat flooded Mason at the memories of him calling Adeline his sister. He'd been repulsed using the word, his feelings toward her at the time nothing of the sort. But she'd been eighteen, so young and innocent, and there was no way he could allow himself to kiss her back. He had been twenty-two, pursuing a career in politics, and she was simply too young.

Looking into her cool blue eyes, he could see the truth written there. Her fingers squeezed together, and she shook them in front of her, like she was jerking herself out of a memory.

"Tell me, please, Adeline. If I'm not the reason you've stayed away, then what is?" Dread filled him with each word he spoke. What could have been so terrible to have made her stay away all this time?

"I've avoided telling you this, and I imagine really that we've both been avoiding each other over what happened all those years ago. But my mom saw me kiss you, and she told Dad. The following day, I overheard them in the study discussing it, how they were saying they would need to keep us apart. I thought that meant my kissing you was going to impact the relationship you had with them, and I felt terrible, so I confronted them."

He reached out and cupped her hands in his larger ones. Her breath was laboured, like what she was going to tell him next was being dredged from down deep.

"I told them it was all me, that you were the innocent party. Dad was so furious with me, his face filled with revulsion at the thought that I'd kissed you. All because of his career. What if this leaked? How would it make Senator Jeffery Miller look if his daughter was having a relationship with her foster brother, under his roof? What would his constituents think?"

Her words were soaked with bitterness. She pulled her hands away, wrapping them around her torso like she was attempting to physically hold herself together. He knew what rejection from parents felt like. His had left him at the group home, saying they couldn't afford to keep him. It hurt him to think of it, but he'd come to terms with it, hoping that he'd eased the burden on them. He couldn't be too upset about it, given where he'd ended up. But Adeline's hurt must run so much deeper. How could her father have chosen his career over her innocent feelings? At such a crucial age in her life, no less. It was no wonder she'd walked away and never looked back.

"I'm so sorry, Adeline."

He stepped into her personal space, wrapping his arms around her and just held her. Damp spread on his shoulder, and he realized she was crying, her body jerking with the effort to try doing so quietly.

Anger tore through him. Anger on her behalf, that she'd spent all these years alone, feeling she needed to shun her family because of her father's political career. The guilt on her father's face at dinner the other night now made sense. Mason was wrong, it wasn't Adeline who should be reaching out to her father, it should be Jeffery apologising to Adeline.

"Adeline, I know we said we'd talk more after the festival is over, but I don't want to wait. Let me take you out to dinner tonight, on a date?"

He felt Adeline stiffen in his arms, and she took a step back, her tear-stained face breaking a little bit more of him on the inside.

"I can't, Mason. I appreciate you hearing me out, and all the support you've given me this week, but my life is in New York. And I have every intention of returning to it once this festival is over. A date between us will just complicate that."

Hurt punched into his heart. "So, the kiss the other day... you didn't feel what I felt?"

"Oh, Mason, of course I felt our connection, you know I did. But I just can't do this with you. Don't you understand?"

"No, I don't. We're both older now, we don't live under the same roof. There's nothing that's standing between us other than a short flight. I think we really have something between us, that could be the real deal. Don't you think that deserves to be delved into? I could come to you, or vice versa. If it works, and I really think it will, I'll look to relocate to New York for the next election. It's a tough state, but I'm sure I could give it a red-hot go. Please, Adeline, I have feelings for you, and I want to see if we can make this work."

"That's just it, you're already making decisions based around your political career. Which you should, but I can't involve myself in that again."

"So, you want me to give up politics? Is that what it's going to take?" The thought jarred slightly, but not as badly as the thought of losing Adeline again.

"No! That's not what I'm saying. Mason, I can't be with someone who is so politically focused; we're just two different. We want different things. I want nothing to do with politics. It ruined my life once, I won't let it in again."

Stabbing pain sliced through his heart, but he didn't stop pushing. Couldn't stop pushing.

"Not even for me?"

* * *

She hated that he'd asked that. The love she felt for Mason was still there, resounding through her every thought and feeling, but it was just too risky. Mason deserved someone who would embrace his career, and she deserved someone who would always put her first.

"I'm sorry, Mason, but I have to go. The event is tomorrow. I hope the bill goes your way, I really do."

Placing a light kiss against his cheek, she breathed in his scent one last time and then walked away. For good.

12

———

*D*eflated didn't come close to how Mason was feeling. He sat in his skyline-view apartment, the drink he'd made untouched. The sun was slowly dipping, so he knew he'd been sitting there a while.

Snippets of his conversation with Adeline swirled like a discombobulated mess in his head.

How could Jeffery have done that to her? Said those things? Politics were important, sure, but nothing compared to love and family...

He had put his heart out there for Adeline to take, and she'd left it sitting in his hand. He understood her wariness. After what she'd been through? It made sense she'd be nervous around anything to do with politics, but he wasn't her dad. She hadn't even given him a chance to prove that. He'd spent the past week trying to show her how he'd be there for her. At the time, he'd just thought he was trying to settle a guilt trip he'd laid on himself, but deep down, he'd always known it was more than that. *She* was more than that to him.

Had he been waiting for her to come back? Waiting until

it had been the right time? He didn't know. What he did know was that he wasn't ready to give up fighting. Not yet.

Picking up the glass soaked with condensation, he walked into the kitchen and dumped its contents down the sink. It was time to go visit Jeffery and Clarise. Now that he knew the whole truth, well, even if Adeline still wanted nothing to do with him, he could ensure they understood how much they'd lost.

* * *

Standing at the coffee shop across from her temporary office, Adeline took a sip of scalding hot coffee. She felt the burn, but it barely registered.

Sleep hadn't really happened the following evening. She wanted to blame the rain, which had hammered on and off for half the night. The hotel room she'd been staying at had views over the Tidal Basin. The lashing of water against the surface would normally have been hypnotic to watch, but currently she hated the rain.

She hated the fact she couldn't control it.

The past ten years she'd worked really hard to ensure everything about her life was in control, her control. She'd never put herself in a position where someone else's opinion could crush her, she'd put a blanket over anything political or family related in her life, and she'd been perfectly fine.

Her whole body ached at the realization that it had all been a total lie, a realization that had come to her around 2 A.M. She wasn't fine. She'd been coasting, pretending. Hiding her head in the sand like a camel.

She missed her parents. Even her dad, even after the choice he'd made. She still missed them. And she missed Mason. There was an emptiness within her, and she had no idea how she'd fill it again. Had she blown her chance with him for good?

The rain should have kept her occupied with worrying over the event, but she couldn't even bring herself to do that. She had until midday to make the final call. The backup location was all set up in case they had to go there. Signs and communication were prepped for any last-minute changes. But regardless, the joy she'd felt in achieving this goal...it had dimmed. It was still there, but instead of glowing bright like a firework, it was now so dull it was like the batteries were on their last legs.

One week, that's all it had taken for her feelings for Mason to ignite and burn brighter than ever. She barely knew him, the adult him. But was that really true? He'd gone above and beyond for her this week. When he should have been racing around trying to fix his own problems, he'd helped her. He'd put her first, over his career.

He'd stood before her, asking for a chance to make this work between them, and she'd said no. All the dreams she'd never put into words were before her yesterday afternoon, and she said no...

What was wrong with her?

Her phone pinged. A picture appeared on the screen for a moment, indicating an incoming message from Mason. Her heart leapt. Diving at the phone, she swiped to bring the message up and was rewarded with a radar image from the National Weather Service. It showcased blue skies for the whole day.

The light within her dimmed. While the weather news was great, what she'd wanted was words. Contact. Anything from Mason.

But that was silly. Because she'd made her decision already, hadn't she?

* * *

Adeline stood at the top of the stairs of the Jefferson Memorial Building. The pontoon before her glittered with dancers, swirls of colour that moved in unison. The music was eerie in its beauty, the modern ballet matching each chord of the live band. Projectors were set up, streaming the footage live, some with backgrounds of picturesque images from Japan and Washington.

Glancing about her, she felt happy to see so many faces enraptured with what they were seeing. The shores of the Tidal Basin were lined with people, bodies poking out of the sea of pink that floated above them. It was a celebration of everything the Festival stood for, and people were loving it.

She'd done it.

Except the emptiness still consumed her.

People shifted, making way for someone excusing their way through. Adeline wobbled on the stiletto heels she wore as Mason and her parents wove their way to her side. Her mom pulled her into a hug, whispering how proud she was, before focusing again on the show before them.

Adeline struggled to make sense of the situation. Her dad was holding flowers, which he awkwardly shoved in her direction before returning his gaze forward.

Burying her face in the blooms, she soaked in the sweet perfume, anything rather than look at Mason. Why was he here? She'd broken her own rules and had looked up Congress to see what time the vote was occurring. It should be on right now. Why wasn't Mason there? Was it over already? It wasn't a long trip from Capitol Hill but traffic around this area was manic today, the official close of the festival.

Mason shifted around behind her to stand on her other side.

She felt his breath at her ear before he whispered, "It's breathtaking."

Her head swivelled to look at him. They were standing so close that she could hear his breathing now. For some reason, she'd expected him to have his gaze focused on the dancers, but it was directly on her.

Heat stole up her cheeks, and she smiled, her lips stretching far wider than they had in a long time. The butterflies she'd expected to have prior to the concert now took flight in her belly.

The show continued for another twenty minutes. It wasn't long, but videos of the performance would continue to play on the big screens around the gardens for the rest of the day. When it ended, she allowed herself the first full breath she'd taken all day, letting it out long and slow.

"Adeline, can I talk to you for a moment?"

People were bustling around them. Everyone looked happy, discussions were lively. She wasn't sure she'd just heard those words. Her dad wanted to talk to her?

"Sure, perhaps we should find somewhere a little less crowded."

They moved in the general direction of the path along the basin, and Adeline hoped she could avoid any of the committee right now. She could feel her phone buzzing, and knew she'd need to take some calls soon, but right now she wanted to hear what her dad had to say.

The crowds started to thin, and she noticed Mason and her mom hung back a little.

"I want to apologise."

Adeline waited. This felt too momentous to interrupt. She didn't need to ask what he was apologising for.

"Darling, I was wrong. I never should have said those things to you. At the time, I thought my career was the all-important thing. I thought you'd come back eventually, but over time I realized the damage I'd done was irreparable, and by then I didn't know where to start to fix anything."

"This seems like a good place to me. All you had to do was pick up the phone and call." She kept her tone neutral, not prepared to give any of her feelings away just yet.

"I know. But it wasn't until Mason came to see me that I realized how badly I'd treated you."

"Mason?"

"Yes, Mason. He insisted we come today, though I want you to know your mother and I were already planning to come."

A tear slid down her cheek, the light breeze clinging to its cool path. Another joined it. Silently, they dripped off her chin. She swallowed at the dryness in her mouth.

"Did you like it?"

She watched her father huff out a deep breath and then smile.

"Yes, Adeline, I liked it a lot. You should be proud of what you achieved today. I am...proud of what you achieved today."

It felt like she'd waited a long time to hear those words from her father. He gave her arm a quick rub, his version of an embrace, and then walked off, leaving her stunned. It was the only word for it. It hadn't been much, but she could feel deep down that this was the turning point she'd needed with her parents.

She'd taken a lot of time last night to dwell on the events of ten years ago. To go over what her parents had said and how she'd reacted. They hadn't told her she had to leave. Yes, her father had focused on his career and not what inner turmoil he was creating for his emotional eighteen-year-old daughter. But she'd never stopped to think about it from her parents' side. At eighteen...well, it really hadn't been the right time. She'd needed to grow up, and today, she finally felt like she could set herself free from the restrictions she'd placed on herself.

"Dad, Mom?" Her parents were walking away together, but both turned in unison at the sound of her voice. "I love you, both of you."

Her words were met with matching smiles of hope, her mother looking on the verge of tears before her dad pulled her along.

Mason stood a few steps away, his hands in his pockets, observing with his usual half-smile. He took a step closer to her and then stopped.

"Seems like things are on the up with your parents." Was his smile just a little smug?

"It would seem so, yes. Thank you." She took a step in his direction.

"You don't need to thank me. Consider it my cherry on top."

His left foot shifted, tapping the ground and then stepping towards her again.

Adeline smiled; she couldn't help it. After all the help he'd given her this week, it seemed he'd also orchestrated an apology from her dad. It went well beyond a cherry on top; this was the whole ice cream shop, chocolate shop, and cherry orchard.

Her next step would bring her right before him, entering his personal space. Having him stand next to her during the show had felt so right. The emptiness she'd been experiencing melted away. He was her missing piece.

"I have one more question, and then I'll leave you alone." Mason's tone was serious.

She stepped forward. "Ask away."

"Why this festival? What is it about this festival that you love?"

Adeline smiled, that was an easy answer to a question she'd been hoping Mason would never ask. Except now, she knew he deserved this answer. And they deserved each other.

"Because it was where we went the day you arrived, and you took my hand and held it for the whole time we walked along the path. You listened to me babble, and not once did you say a thing. But you smiled. And I fell in love with you."

"Can I take your hand again now, Adeline? And never let it go?"

Adeline felt a light thud on her shoulder, then another wetter one on her forehead. Tipping her head back, she stared at the pink sea above her, the wind whipping delicate petals into a flurry around them. Rain droplets turned to drizzle, soaking both her and Mason in minutes. A giggle escaped her before she looked at Mason again.

"You can take my hand, and I guess I should probably tell you you've also got my heart. Always have and always will."

She didn't wait for him to move, instead she pressed her lips to his. Not the kiss of an immature teenager infatuated with a boy, but a kiss of passion, of love, and of knowledge that he loved her back.

The End

EXCERPT: A KISS FOR CHRISTMAS EVE

-I-

Cara Hewitt surveyed the bar around her. Possibly not the best place to be at 4 p.m. on a random Tuesday afternoon, but she was giving herself a well-earned break.

The latest letter was burning a hole in her purse where she'd shoved the dastardly thing. *Proposed rent increases after the pending sale.* She'd sent yet *another* email requesting a response from the guy who was selling.

Cara harrumphed. They were trying to bully their tenants out, and it was highway robbery. This was Cathedral Springs! It might be situated in upstate New York, but it was a far cry from New York City.

There was no way she could sustain her business if this sale went through. Which meant she needed to speak to the man selling the land her shop sat on and stop him. And she had to do it quick smart.

She took a fortifying sip of the crisp dry sherry the bartender kept especially for her. It might be something mostly drunk by little old ladies, but the dry flavor suited her tastes. Plus, the bartender served it in vintage crystal glasses that she'd donated to the bar purely for this purpose, so it was a win-win all around.

The door tinkled, and a rush of cold air brought with it the news that someone else had entered.

Glancing over, Cara smiled as her friend Marianne wove her way between the tables and then glided onto a stool opposite. Marianne was every bit the beautiful ballet teacher and even managed to make sitting on a chair look graceful. It would grate if she were not so lovely.

"Is it snowing out?" Cara asked, noting the flecks of snow scattered over her friend's shoulders and beret.

"Just a little. December has well and truly arrived." The other woman smiled. Of course Marianne had a lot to smile about. Her Christmas concert had been spectacular, she'd shacked up with the town's gorgeous loner, Duncan, and the two were due to marry in early spring next year.

Cara was beyond thrilled that Marianne had asked her to keep an eye out for something from her store for her to wear. She'd found the most stunning 1920s off-white silk gown and couldn't wait to show Marianne. The estate salesperson had been thrilled when Cara had wanted to purchase the whole trunk of clothes found in someone's attic. Cara had drooled over the pieces, and whilst the stock put a hefty dent in her finances, the inventory was simply too gorgeous to walk away from. The twenties was such an elegant period of fashion...and those hats! She knew she'd probably end up keeping a few pieces for herself.

"Earth to Cara?"

"Sorry?"

"Where did you go?"

"Nineteen twenties. My shipment arrived today. I have news...dun dun *dun.*"

Marianne rolled her eyes at Cara's theatrics. And probably with good reason.

"You found my dress?" Marianne asked with a somewhat knowing grin.

"Oh. How did you know that?"

"Your face just now. You lit up like a Christmas tree. I know how excited you've been about finding me my perfect dress so I put two and two together."

"Of course you did, Miss Smarty Pants. So, do you want to hear about it?"

"No. Let's leave it as a surprise for now." Marianne's lips curved into a dreamy smile, and Cara knew that the swaths of silk would look perfect with her delicate features and dancer's body. Duncan was going to have a freaking heart attack.

God, I wish I had something like that. More recently, Cara's desire for a connection, to meet someone, was starting to invade her thoughts on a daily basis. Too bad there wasn't anyone in town who fit that bill.

"I heard the block owner has arrived in town," said Marianne. "Apparently, he grew up here. Has he answered any of the letters you've sent?"

"No. Which is frustrating. But if he's here, maybe I can ask him in person. Surely he must see that selling to that stupid building company will only result in bad news for Cathedral Springs. Who on earth could afford to buy a mid-rise condo around here anyway? And who in their right mind would want to? I think it's just bogus."

Cara could feel herself getting riled up. For years she'd searched for the perfect town, the perfect place to set up her shop and put down roots. Actually make a home for herself. And now that her little enterprise was starting to become established, some unknown man was threatening to rip that dream to shreds.

But no way was she going down without a fight.

This Mr. Aimes needed to understand that selling to the Compton Group was an absolute mistake. Sure, he'd make loads more money, but where was his heart? He grew up here—he should know what this town was about.

The door swung inwards again, this time revealing a well-dressed man bundled in a wool coat. Ice and snow swept in at his feet before he was able to slam the door closed behind him. A large scarf sat around his neck, and she knew just by sight that it was high-quality. Probably cashmere.

He looked around, his eyes searching and discarding as he went. She wondered what it would be like to be on the receiving end of that intense gaze, being the person he was searching for. Her heart pinged a little, and she focused on the drink before her. What an odd thought to have about a complete stranger. On the plus side, it had zapped away her anger at the elusive Mr. Aimes.

She snuck another glance at the stranger, noting he took off the coat and scarf before he strode over to the bar.

Unusual for a complete stranger to be in this run-down bar. Tourists who did happen upon this town usually chose to go to the more upmarket wine bar over on Lake Street.

Mr. Handsome Stranger ordered a beer, before taking a seat against the bar. He focused on the TV, which, predictably, held recaps of last night's Rangers' win. Ice hockey wasn't her thing, but then she'd never really stayed long enough in one place to form any sort of sports follow-ing. Perhaps ice hockey could *become* her thing? Just as the thought occurred, two burly men on the screen flung their gloves to the ground and started punching each other.

Hmm. Or perhaps not.

"Marianne," she asked her friend. "What's your sport?"

Marianne followed her gaze, glancing over her shoulder to see the television. "Not ice hockey. I love watching ice dancing though. Why do you ask?"

Before Cara could answer, Marianne's phone lit up, a happy jingle giving away the caller. Cara tried not to feel envious as Marianne answered the call, her friend's voice softening with love as she answered her fiancé's query. Those two were made for each other, but it didn't stop Cara's heart letting out a spurt of longing. *One day.*

Her mind and eyes drifted back towards Mr. Handsome Stranger but stopped dead when she caught him looking right at her. His smile was inviting. Taking a deep breath, Cara decided to take a chance. Why not go say hello? What was the worst that could happen?

STAY CONNECTED

Never miss a new release or give away! Sign up to Jayne's newsletter here to stay in the loop.

And if you loved this book, please take a moment to leave a review once you're done.

Thank you!

ALSO BY JAYNE KINGSLEY

SINGLE TITLES

Loving Lucas

THE STENISH ROYALS

Sweet Royal Romance

#0.5 Finding A Forever Love (Novella Prequel)

#1 Tailored for Her Prince

#2 Her Convenient Playboy Prince

#3 Guarding His Runaway Princess

FOUR SEASONS OF ROMANCE

Sweet Novella Reads

#1 Cherry On Top (Spring)

#2 A Kiss for Christmas Eve (Winter)

www.ingramcontent.com/pod-product-compliance
Lightning Source LLC
Chambersburg PA
CBHW030438120726
47903CB00003B/1017